The Graveyard Hounds by Vi Hughes

illustrations by **Christina Leist**

Vancouver • London

To Alison, Michael and Andrew who know
the joy that dogs bring to our lives—VH

To my girlfriends overseas, thanks for
all the good energy—CL

TABLE OF CONTENTS

CHAPTER 1

The Storm

A small black squirrel poked its head out of the branches and chattered at Casey and Sheba. The two dogs spotted it and barked loudly. The squirrel scampered down the tree, and the dogs took off after it, disappearing behind the school.

"Oh no!" Mike said to Annie. "Trouble!"

Mike scanned the windows. He expected to see the principal, Mr. Mulligan, staring down his glasses at them. Mr. Mulligan was always popping up to catch kids the instant they broke a school rule.

A slight movement caught Mike's eye. Someone was watching them, but it wasn't the principal. It was Mr. Duffy, the new school custodian. He was smoking a pipe and looking out of one of the class-room windows. When he saw Mike looking back at him, he quickly closed the blinds.

A sudden wind scattered leaves across the ground. Lightning flashed and thunder rumbled. Heavy drops of rain rattled onto the tin slide like nails on a coffin, sending shivers up Mike's neck. Casey came racing back.

"It's okay. Come here, boy!" Mike called.

Dripping with rain, the big dog stopped beside him. Annie and Mike called for Sheba, but their voices were lost in a roll of thunder. They called again. Finally, the black and white sheltie came running toward them with her head down.

"Sheba!" Annie yelled. "Good girl!"

"We're going home now, Casey," Mike said.

As Mike and Annie turned to go, a bolt of lightning lit the sky above the playground, followed by another wave of rolling thunder.

"That was close," Mike said.

Casey barked frantically. Sheba looked like she was barking too, but Mike noticed something odd.

"Annie," Mike said. "There's something wrong with Sheba."

"What?"

"She's not making any noise when she barks."

"She's not?" Annie asked. She held Sheba close to her as the storm raged. "Maybe you didn't hear her barking over the thunder."

"Maybe. Anyway, we'd better get home," Mike said.

They started running, heads lowered against the pounding rain. As they approached their apartment building, Mike saw his big brother, Ritchie, holding the lobby door open.

"Come on, you guys!" Ritchie yelled. "Hurry up!"

Casey bounded inside and shook like crazy, splattering water and dirt everywhere. Sheba saw

Ritchie and barked. But what everyone heard was a peculiar huffing sound.

"What's up with Sheba?" Ritchie asked as they piled into the stairwell.

"I don't know," Annie said. "But I want to get her home."

Mike and Annie both lived on the second floor. When they got to her apartment, Annie took out her key, opened the door and shooed Sheba inside. "See you tomorrow," she said.

Mike wanted to say something—to ask about Sheba—but it was too late. Annie had closed the door.

Weird, thought Mike. ❧

CHAPTER 2

Spooky News

Mike stood shivering as Ritchie opened their door. Casey squeezed between the two boys and burst into the apartment.

Mike could see his mom and dad sitting at the kitchen table watching the news on television.

Here it comes, he thought. He waited for the lecture about being out in the rain and letting the dog drip water all over.

But his mom and dad didn't even look up. They were glued to the television. Mike took off his wet jacket and looked over to see what they were watching.

The weatherman and the news reporter were in the middle of a story. "Let's have a look at those pictures again," the weatherman said.

Images of the storm flashed onto the screen. Trees had toppled over onto power lines and roads, and houses had been hit by falling branches. A fire was raging in the old church beside the churchyard. Flames and black smoke rose out of the church roof into the dark sky.

"It's unusual for us to get such severe storms with such heavy winds and so much thunder and lightning," the weatherman said. "No other towns are reporting anything like this. And what's more, this storm doesn't appear anywhere on the satellite photos. It's very strange."

"Well," the news reporter responded, "it *is* the season when strange things happen. The spooky season. Halloween is only a few days away."

"Button up your overcoats, folks!" exclaimed the weatherman.

The news and weather were just ending when the telephone rang. Ritchie answered it and came into the kitchen holding the receiver. "Mom," he said, "it's for you. It's Annie's mom."

Mike's mom took the phone. "Hello? What? How odd," she said. "Yes, please let us know as soon as you can." She put down the phone and turned to face everyone. "Something very curious has happened," she said.

"To Annie?" Mike's dad asked.

"No. To Sheba."

"What?" he asked.

"This sounds crazy, but Sheba has lost her bark."

"Like when you have a cold or something?" Ritchie asked.

His mom shook her head. "No," she said.

"What, then?" Ritchie asked.

"We don't know. But Annie's mom said Sheba looked like she was trying to yip and couldn't get the sound out. You know how she barks."

"Yeah," Mike said. So something *was* wrong.

"Mrs. Lee said that she's going to take Sheba to see the vet tomorrow," his mom said. "She'll tell us what she finds out."

彡彡

In bed that night, Mike listened to the wind and rain slapping the windows and pounding the roof. It was so dark he could barely make out Casey's big black shape on the floor. Mike could hear him snoring and making muffled woofs. Casey had always been a noisy sleeper.

Do dogs dream? Do dogs talk in their sleep? Mike wondered.

He fell asleep thinking about Sheba losing her bark. It was weird.

But the next day at school, things got even weirder. ❧

CHAPTER 3

Rules and Violations

"I wonder what's going on here," Mike said to Annie as they crossed the road to the school grounds. Workmen were unloading wire fencing from a huge truck. A crowd had gathered in front of the adventure playground. Mike stood on tiptoe to see what they were looking at. He caught a glimpse of the top of the slide. It looked strangely off-kilter.

"Let's get closer so we can see," Annie said.

Mike and Annie squeezed their way through the crowd to get a better look. They found a spot beside Mr. Mulligan and Mr. Duffy, who were talking quietly.

Mike heard Mr. Mulligan say, "It's not bad luck. It's a coincidence."

A workman was talking to the parents and teachers standing around. "Serious fire here," the man said. "Must have been last night. The whole darn thing's burned up. Keep the kids off it. We're closing it off 'til it's fixed." The man began unwinding yellow caution tape.

Annie and Mike were close enough now to see what had caused the commotion. The entire adventure playground was in ruins. The wooden beams and posts were charred and black. The plastic tunnels had melted into sagging shapes. The metal slide hung there, lopsided and useless. The top wooden platform had burned away.

The workmen were setting up a fence around the ruined playground as the warning bell rang for students to go inside. Mike and Annie hung back until everyone had gone into the school.

"We were here last night," Annie said.

"Yeah," Mike said as he gazed at the metal slide. He remembered how the rain had rattled down on it when Sheba and Casey chased the squirrel.

The second bell rang, and Mike and Annie hurried off into the school building. As they walked through the basement, Mike noticed Mr. Duffy standing near his office door. He didn't move as Mike and Annie filed past, but Mike could feel his eyes following them. "'Tis bad luck," he heard Mr. Duffy mutter. "Very bad luck."

Just before recess, an announcement came over the public address system. "Mike Andrews, come to the office please." It was Mr. Mulligan's voice. When

Mike stood up, everyone in the class turned to look at him. The principal's office! That meant trouble.

As he left the classroom, Mike wondered which one of Mr. Mulligan's rules he had broken. He considered them carefully as he walked down the long hallway to the office. It wasn't as if Mike had never done anything wrong. One time, he had climbed up the basketball pole but couldn't get down. He had got stuck swinging from the hoop when the bell rang, and Mr. Mulligan had to come outside and rescue him. Mr. Mulligan had said he was impulsive—goofy even.

And then there was the ladder incident. Mike had been waiting outside the music room for Annie and noticed a ladder against the wall. He wondered, at the time, where a ladder on the top floor of a school would go. Did the school have an attic? What would be up there? He never found out. Mr. Mulligan stopped him just as he was pushing open the trap door in the ceiling.

But those incidents were way in the past. For the life of him, Mike couldn't think of what he had done now. Part of the problem was that there were so many rules, he had no idea which one he might have broken. And Mr. Mulligan made new rules all the time. Every time Mr. Mulligan thought of one, he posted it on the wall. Mike read them as he walked along. Which rule was it this time?

THE SPEED LIMIT IS SLOW.

Not that one, Mike thought.

GO OUTSIDE AT RECESS AND NOON. RAIN MAKES YOU GROW.

I always play outside.

KEEP TO THE RIGHT.

Oh. Mike scooted over to the other side of the hallway.

Some of the rules even had illustrations. Just before he reached the office, Mike passed his personal favourite. He had drawn the picture for this rule as a punishment during detention: PEE IN THE TOILET, **NOT** ON THE PLANTS.

ᕤᕙ

Mike sat in the small area outside the principal's office waiting for Mrs. Williams, the school secretary, to tell him when to enter. He could hear the clock ticking the seconds until recess.

Mike knew that you could go into that office and not come out for a very long time. Sometimes a kid lost a whole recess sitting under the big lights in the principal's office. What were the words Mr. Mulligan used? *Oh yeah—sit and reflect on the rules and violations,* Mike thought.

The bell went. Recess already. More long seconds passed. *Maybe it has something to do with the dogs,* Mike thought. Had Mr. Mulligan popped up yesterday without them knowing and seen the dogs running around loose on the school grounds? Mike didn't think so. But maybe Mr. Duffy had ratted on them. *That's possible*, Mike thought.

He could hear all the other kids having fun outside while he sat inside wasting his valuable recess minutes. He poked through the magazines on the little table and worked on his excuses to make sure they sounded sincere.

I'm sorry. I got mixed up. It wasn't my fault. I did it by accident. He did it first. The leash slipped out of my hand. Honest.

A kid needed to be ready.

At last, Mrs. Williams said, "You can go in now, Mike."

Mike walked to the principal's door, took a deep breath and turned the knob. ❧

CHAPTER 4

The Principal's Office

M r. Mulligan was hanging up the phone. He swivelled his chair around and gestured for Mike to sit down. As always, Mr. Mulligan lifted his feet off the floor as he swivelled. Mike always thought it was weird that a grown-up would do that. When the chair stopped moving, Mr. Mulligan planted his feet on the floor, folded his hands under his chin and looked at the boy over the rim of his glasses.

Mike squirmed in his chair.

Mr. Mulligan tapped his fingers. "I know that you bring your dog to the playground, Mike."

That wasn't a question, so Mike waited.

"You were here last night."

Was a question coming? Mike knew not to say too much. Sometimes Mr. Mulligan didn't know anything and he tricked kids into saying stuff. He was good at that. A kid had to watch what he said.

Mr. Mulligan continued, "Were you here last night, Mike?"

"Yes." What else *could* he say?

"Was Annie with you?" Mike could see from the principal's face that he knew that Annie had been there.

"Yeah."

"Her dog too?"

"Yeah."

"Did you see what happened? What started the fire?"

"No."

"Did you see anyone else?"

"No."

"No one?"

"Oh, just Mr. Duffy."

"Mr. Duffy?"

"Yeah, he was looking out of the window."

Mr. Mulligan sat there looking at Mike for a long time. Then he asked, "What kind of dog do you have, Mike?"

"I...I don't know what kind of dog Casey is...maybe a Lab."

"Maybe a Lab?"

"Maybe."

"Does Casey bark a lot?"

"No."

"Not bark? A big dog like that?"

"Not really. We live in an apartment. He has to be quiet."

"Does he ever bark?"

"Yes, sometimes."

Mike was puzzled. Where was this heading?

"When does he bark?" Mr. Mulligan asked.

"When we go outside."

They sat quietly. Mr. Mulligan, hands folded, kept looking at Mike.

Mike tried hard not to look at Mr. Mulligan. He made his eyes look at the bookshelves behind the desk. There were lots of things there: dog puppets, Clifford the Big Red Dog and Goofy, and different kinds of noses—clown noses and pig noses, and a nose with glasses and a moustache. There were some books too, but Mike couldn't read the titles from where he was sitting.

He heard Mr. Mulligan draw a deep breath.

Here comes the lecture, Mike thought.

Just then the phone rang. Startled, Mike sat bolt upright in the chair.

Mr. Mulligan never once looked away from the boy as he picked up the telephone, listened for a moment and said, "Yes. Tell him I'll be with him in a moment." He hung up.

Mike got his excuses ready.

But what Mr. Mulligan said surprised him. "Mike, we can't have dogs loose on the school playground. They bark. They poop. They jump on the kindergarten kids and scare them, particularly the big dogs. People get really mad. Especially the grandmas. You should hear them. They've yelled at me. They've chased me. They've hit me with their umbrellas." Mr. Mulligan scratched the top of his head.

"I have a dog myself, Mike," he said, picking up a small photograph from his desk and holding it out for Mike to see. "I used to bring him to school when I worked nights and weekends. You know, for company. But I stopped doing that to show kids that *I* follow the school rules too."

Mike relaxed. It didn't sound like he was in trouble.

Mr. Mulligan pointed to his bookshelf. "Take a look at the books there, Mike. I have a lot of books about dogs. I like dogs."

Mike walked over to the bookshelf, pretending to be interested. He could see there were lots of books about dogs. But what really struck him were the other books—books about magic and some strange titles he couldn't quite make sense of.

"I don't know what caused the fire on the playground," Mr. Mulligan said. "The fire chief is waiting to talk to me, and he might have some answers. For the time being, you have to stay away from there and play somewhere else."

Mr. Mulligan lifted his feet and turned his chair around. That was the signal Mike could leave. "And, Mike, look after that dog of yours," Mr. Mulligan said, with his back turned.

When Mike stepped into the outer office, he saw the fire chief poking through the magazines.

The bell rang. Recess was over. Annie was waiting for him outside the classroom. "What was that all about?" she asked.

"It's about yesterday," he said. "He knows we were here with the dogs. I'll bet he calls you to the office too."

After school, Annie and Mike compared information. "It's strange," Annie said. "Mr. Mulligan asked me if Sheba barked a lot too. I wonder what that has to do with the fire."

"Did he tell you how the fire started?" Mike asked.

"He said lightning struck the adventure playground. The fire chief told him."

"Could've been us burning," Mike said.

They rushed home, anxious to learn about Sheba's visit to the vet.

The news was not good. ❖

CHAPTER 5

An Interesting Small Town Phenomenon

Mike followed Annie as she opened the door, stepped in and called out, "Mom? Sheba?"

Mrs. Lee was sitting at the kitchen table. Sheba lay beside her on the floor. The dog got up to greet Annie and Mike when she saw them. Mike knelt down to pat her.

"What did the vet say, Mom?" Annie asked.

"Sheba has lost her bark," Mrs. Lee said. "When Dr. Stephanie examined her, she found Sheba was

perfectly healthy. But her bark has disappeared—just gone. Poof!" She snapped her fingers. "Dr. Stephanie can't understand it."

Everyone looked down at Sheba, who wagged her tail and looked up at them. She opened her mouth and tried to bark. Out puffed a whisper. "Huh-ur." It sounded like a tiny motor revving up.

"Dr. Stephanie said she doesn't know if her bark will come back," Mrs. Lee said. "It might. It might not...and there's something else."

"What else, Mom?" Annie asked.

"The vet said that Sheba is not even her first case. Dr. Stephanie said she has treated other dogs since the storm and all the dogs have the same symptoms." Mrs. Lee looked over at Mike. "Check Casey when you get home, Mike," she said.

Yk

When Mike opened his door, Casey rushed over to greet him. The dog snuffled and woofed softly as Mike got him a treat. *Nothing wrong here,* Mike thought.

The family sat down to watch the news.

"Well, folks," the weatherman said, "there's a bizarre twist to the story we've been following about severe storms in the area. And it's very strange indeed. We know that many dogs are afraid of thunder and lightning. Apparently, some of the dogs in town have been scared out of their barks. Dr. Stephanie, our local veterinarian, tells us that dogs are being brought to her clinic with laryngitis. These dogs cannot bark. Otherwise healthy—vocal cords intact—no signs of mistreatment. She can't explain it."

"What's even stranger," the news reporter said, "is that this doesn't seem to be happening anywhere else. No one in any other town has reported a dog with laryngitis. Thunder, lightning and silent dogs. Spooky stuff."

He turned to the weatherman. "Are any more storms headed this way?"

"Not according to the satellite. No storms in sight," the weatherman said. "But I'd keep my umbrella handy and my pets indoors, just in case."

"What we have here is an interesting small town phenomenon, folks," the news reporter said. "Mysterious, ghostly weather patterns, dogs with no barks and Halloween coming up. Stay tuned."

The news signed off with eerie music and a camera sweep of the small town, showing the damage to the school grounds, the town streets and the little church with the cemetery. The church was barely recognizable since the fire. But the bell steeple was still standing, like a ghost rising above the smoke and ashes. The camera paused at the entrance to the graveyard and zoomed in on the smouldering gateposts. The fire had swooped up each side of the gate, burning the posts. They looked like huge black daggers cutting through the haze.

Mike shivered at the sight.

CHAPTER 6

Weird Saturday

On Saturday morning, it was overcast and cold, but not stormy. Annie, Mike and Ritchie took Sheba and Casey to the basketball court. Annie sat against the school building, counting the lucky stars her grandma had brought her from China and watching Mike and Ritchie shoot hoops. Casey and Sheba chased the bouncing ball as the boys wove around them. Mike shot the ball and missed the basket time after time.

Ritchie yelled, "You gotta work on that aim, goofball!"

Mike, tired of losing to his brother, called out to Annie, "Let's go see what's happening at the playground!"

Ritchie put the earphones of his iPod into his ears and stayed on the court, shooting hoops by himself. Annie and Mike ran off with the dogs.

The playground equipment was now completely surrounded by a high, wire fence.

"That fence must be ten feet high," Mike said.

"Yeah. But hey, look up there." Annie pointed at an orange basketball in the branches of the huge oak tree next to the fence. The ball was wedged tightly on a branch hanging over the playground.

"Let's get it down," Mike said.

They tried shaking the tree to get the ball down, but it wouldn't budge. Mike turned and looked at his brother in the distance.

"Hey, Ritchie! Come and help!" he yelled. But Ritchie couldn't hear and continued shooting baskets.

"I'll go up and get it," Mike said.

Mike started climbing the tree, but had trouble getting a foothold on the trunk. The dogs jumped up and down, snapping at the twigs that fell away. Casey barked and Sheba tried to, but made no sound.

Finally, Mike got high enough to grab the branch that was holding the ball. *Oh no*, he thought as he looked down. He felt a little dizzy.

"Be careful!" Annie yelled. The branch cracked, and Mike's foot slipped. He scrambled down.

"That was goofy," Annie said.

"Yeah," Mike said, smiling.

"Let's get something to throw at the ball," Annie suggested. They looked around and found some sticks and pebbles and a round Tupperware container.

They took turns throwing the sticks and pebbles, but the ball would not budge.

"I don't think this Tupperware is heavy enough to knock the ball out," Annie said. "Let's put something in it. That might work."

Annie picked up some rocks, and Mike pulled at the lid of the container. Just as the lid came off, they heard a familiar bark—high-pitched and yippy.

"Sheba, was that you?" Annie asked in surprise. She looked at Sheba, who perked up her ears and looked at her.

At that moment, someone grabbed Mike's hand and snatched the Tupperware container away.

It was Mr. Duffy. He stood beside them, holding his pipe in one hand and the Tupperware container in the other. "Thank you very much," he said in a slow, rumbling voice as he slipped his pipe into his pocket. "I was wondering where this got to. Must have dropped it." He snapped the lid on tight and tucked the container into another pocket. He looked closely at Mike and Annie. "I saw you trying to get the basketball down. 'Twas lucky for you that you didn't fall off the branch onto the other side of the fence. 'Twould have been a deal of trouble to get you out."

Sheba sniffed at Mr. Duffy's pocket. He stepped back.

"Good day," he said. "I have to be off. There's work to be done." He walked toward the school and then turned back for a moment. "Yes, 'twould have been bad luck all right if you had landed on the other side of the fence."

Annie and Mike watched him disappear around the corner of the building.

"Mike," Annie whispered. "Did you hear that bark?"

"I think so," he said. "Maybe. I don't know. Mr. Duffy grabbed my hand. It freaked me out."

"I'm sure I heard Sheba bark."

"Huh? What do you mean? Is she better?"

"I don't know," Annie said. "Let's find out."

Annie and Mike started running toward the basketball court. The dogs followed. Casey woofed it up, but Sheba could only make those huffing noises. Mike and Annie stopped and leaned against the school. The dogs lay down beside them.

"Sheba still isn't making any sound," Annie said, "so where did that bark come from?"

"Maybe it was another dog," Mike said.

"Maybe," Annie said. "But I didn't see any other dogs around. Did you?"

Mike shook his head.

"I'm sure that was Sheba's bark," Annie insisted.

"Weird," Mike said.

A bolt of lightning lit up the sky. Thunder boomed. Then, *crack!* Mike and Annie turned back to see the branch Mike had been standing on break away from the oak tree. It fell onto the top of the fence and hung there precariously. The basketball popped out and bounced onto the ground inside the fence.

Sheba and Casey jumped up. Casey barked furiously. Sheba huffed. Ritchie yelled, "C'mon, let's go! Let's move!"

Long before they reached home, the storm had blackened the sky and unleashed the rain, soaking them through and through. 🐾

CHAPTER 7

The Ominous Stranger

Mike's family had regular routines. Watching the news reports was one of them. And now their small town was actually in the news, even the national *and* international news.

This Interesting Small Town Phenomenon was a major story. Mike's dad clicked from station to station to get every detail about the dogs losing their barks.

On the local channel, the news reporter and the weatherman repeated their story about the spooky goings-on. "Keep your eyes open," the news reporter said. "Watch out for anything that appears to be unusual. Or *anyone*, for that matter. There's no explanation for what's been happening." Spooky music came on as the station played clips of the burnt-out church and the damaged playground.

Mike's dad clicked off the television. "Reporters! Just stirring things up. Everything has an explanation. We'll find out soon enough."

Everyone agreed, though, that they should keep an eye on Casey.

Going for a walk on Sunday was another regular routine. "Dogs need exercise," Mike's dad always said. "And big dogs need big exercise." Annie, her mom and Sheba usually joined Mike's family on these walks.

It was a cold, dark, blustery October morning. Mike and Annie braced themselves against the wind as the two families set off to walk around the town, eventually arriving at the school playground.

"Look at that," Mike's dad said as they crossed the street onto the playground. "We've got company." Everyone looked up.

A huge flock of crows had claimed the air space around the school. They were perched along the roof of the school building, on the bare branches of the trees and all along the power lines. Hundreds of crows. Maybe thousands. They were all cawing. Many were being tossed around by the wind. They flapped their wings and swooped, trying to land on something.

Mike knew about the crows. They arrived at the same time every year, flying from a rookery several miles away. What a ruckus they made! And what a mess!

"Cacophonous," Mike's dad said.

"What?" Mike asked.

"Noisy," his dad said.

Mike's dad knew the strangest words. Mike looked up at him. His dad seemed to be thinking about something.

"That's odd," his dad said.

"What?"
Mike asked.

"Look at the adventure playground. There are no crows there."

"Yeah. Weird."

"And there are no crows on that tree. Why would that be?"

"That's the tree the lightning hit."

Then the wind died down. The crows stopped cawing.

It became quiet so suddenly they could hear the voices of the weather: the tree rustling, the branch crackling, the leaves scrunching underfoot. Patches of fog slowly closed in around them. And then, just as slowly, the fog moved away, slithering across the school grounds. As it crept along, a tall thin man emerged from it. The fog swirled around him as he approached.

"Please allow me to introduce myself," the man said, nodding as he spoke. "My name is Mr. Corone. I work for the Unnatural News Network." He handed each of them a card. Mike looked at the man's hand. It looked like a claw. He stared at it while the man spoke.

"This story about the dogs and this little town is making news in faraway places," he said. "I'm here to cover the story." He smiled. "Have any of your dogs been affected by this?"

"Why, yes," said Mrs. Lee. "Our dog has lost her bark." She looked down at Sheba. The man leaned over to look too. The way he leaned was very peculiar, with just his head and neck, like he was pecking at something. Sheba pulled away.

The stranger took out a notepad and began to write. Mrs. Lee pointed to the adventure playground as she explained what else had happened. With jerky nodding movements, the stranger looked at the tree, the damaged play equipment and the school. He made some more notes and finally slipped his notebook and pen into his pocket.

"And this dog?" the stranger asked, pointing at Casey. "Has he been affected by these strange events?"

"Casey's okay," Mike responded quickly. He reached down and held Casey close to him.

Mike's dad studied the card in his hand. "The Unnatural News Network? I've never heard of it."

"Ours is a unique international organization," the man said. "We look for news stories like this one, strange, unusual stories about events and things that cannot be explained naturally. *We* explain them." He smiled again.

Then without speaking to anyone else, he walked away, sliding like a knife into the fog.

Mike stood there wondering if he was the only one who thought the guy was strange.

"Peculiar name for a news network, if you ask me," Mike's dad said.

Mike's mom began walking away. "Let's go home. It's too cold to stand here any longer."

"Will you look at that!" Mike's dad exclaimed. He pointed at the school.

"What?" Mike's mom asked.

"The crows. They're all gone. I didn't even hear them fly away."

⅄⅄

They heard about the crows on the news that night. "Well, we warned you to look out for anything unusual," the news reporter said, "and this is as spooky as it gets. Listeners have been calling all day to say that thousands of crows have been spotted in the graveyard."

"It's an omen," the weatherman said.

"What's an omen?" Mike asked his dad.

"It's a sign that there's trouble ahead," his dad said. "Superstition, that's all." ❧

CHAPTER 8

Knives Are Dangerous

Monday was pumpkin carving day. With Halloween only days away, Mike's class was busy making jack-o'-lanterns. It was messy work. When Miss Walters asked for a volunteer, Mike's hand shot up. To his dismay, she told him to go down to the

custodian's office. She wanted him to ask Mr. Duffy for some containers for the pumpkin seeds and extra garbage bags.

Mike now wished he hadn't volunteered so quickly. But he couldn't *unvolunteer*. Sure, he was glad to be out of class, but he didn't like going to see Mr. Duffy. For one thing, his office was in a dark corner of the basement. For another thing, Mr. Duffy made kids wait forever before he answered their knock.

As he neared Mr. Duffy's office, the rumble of the furnace gave Mike the shivers. He was surprised to see the door ajar. Mike knocked, waited and knocked again, more loudly. As he stood there, he practised what he was going to say. *Miss Walters sent me for some garbage bags and containers for the pumpkin seeds.*

He knocked again, even harder this time. There was still no reply. He wasn't sure what to do. Should he go in?

"Mr. Duffy? Mr. Duffy!" Mike called. Then he took a deep breath and stepped into the room. He looked around. It took a minute for his eyes to adjust to the dim light. There was clutter every-where—little chairs, shopping bags filled with more shopping bags, containers of every size and sort and lots of ice cream pails. But no Mr. Duffy.

Where else could he be? Mike wondered. Then it came to him—the furnace room. If Mr. Duffy was in there, he might not have heard him call. Mike walked over to the furnace room door and knocked three times, loudly.

He heard Mr. Duffy's voice call out, "Who's there?" The next moment he heard the sound of breaking glass and the barking of a dog.

Mike jumped back. *What's going on here?* he wondered. *Does Mr. Duffy have a dog in there?*

"It's Mike," he said loudly, "from Miss Walters' class. She sent me down to get some stuff from you." There was no response. "Mr. Duffy?"

"I'll be with you in a moment," came the reply.

Slowly the door opened, and Mr. Duffy squeezed out, closing the door firmly behind him. "Good afternoon, Mike. What can I do for you?"

Mike blurted out, "Miss Walters sent me for some garbage bags and containers for the pumpkin seeds."

"Ahhh, carving pumpkins then? Is it knives you're using?"

"Yes."

"'Tis bad luck having knives at school! You be careful now."

Mr. Duffy picked up a couple of ice cream pails and stuffed garbage bags into them. He handed them to Mike. "Be careful, now," he repeated.

Mike walked out of the office with the sound of the bark echoing in his ears. It was very weird. He thought that even now he could hear growling in the walls along the hallway.

But that's stupid, he told himself.

When he got back to the classroom, he saw Miss Walters putting a bandage around Annie's hand.

"It's just a small cut," Annie explained. "The knife slipped."

Creepy, Mike thought.

On the walk home, Mike described what had happened in Mr. Duffy's office.

"That doesn't make any sense to me," Annie said. "Mr. Mulligan's got strict rules about no dogs in school. And growling in the walls? Mike, how can that be?"

"It is crazy," Mike agreed. "It's kind of like when you heard Sheba's bark in the playground."

"Gives me goosebumps," Annie said. ❧

CHAPTER 9

Gone Missing

When they got home, Mike and Annie played hockey with the dogs in the alley behind the apartment. Sheba played goalie, her leash tied to the net. She pulled the net around the pavement as Mike and Annie slapped the puck and tried to

score a goal. Casey played offence. He ran around, barked, got into everyone's way and tried to grab the puck.

They had been playing for a while when Casey spotted a black squirrel running down the alley. He barked and took off after it. Sheba followed, dragging the hockey net.

Annie grabbed the net, stopping Sheba, but Casey disappeared around the corner, barking away.

Mike ran after him, following the sound of his barks. They now seemed to be coming from the direction of the school playground. But then the barks stopped. Mike looked around. He was confused. What could have happened? He raced toward the school.

When Mike reached the playground, his heart nearly stopped. Casey was at the foot of the oak tree, under the broken branch that looked like it would fall at any moment. He had his front legs on the tree and was looking up. His jaw was moving furiously as if he was barking. But no sound was coming out. There was no sign of the squirrel. Something else

was sitting high up just below the broken branch. It was a crow.

"Casey!" Mike yelled.

Suddenly, Mr. Duffy stepped out from behind the tree. He was holding a little kid's lunch kit and muttering to himself.

"A crow on the thatch, soon death lifts the latch."

Mr. Duffy stopped muttering when he saw Mike and hurried away. The crow flew off.

Mike grabbed Casey by the collar and looked him over. Casey wagged his tail and made whining movements. But that was all.

Annie came running up with Sheba. Mike blurted out what he had seen.

"Mike, this is exactly how Sheba lost her bark too," Annie said. "Remember? Mr. Duffy was watching out the window. He has something to do with this. I'm sure of it."

"Yeah. Looks like it," Mike agreed. "And remember what I said about the furnace room and the barks I heard?" He looked at the school and then at Annie. "Let's go see what we can find out."

They walked to the back of the school and tried the door. It was locked. They turned to walk to another door but stopped when they heard noises from inside. Someone was coming. They scooted behind the blue recycling container and looped the dog leashes over an iron post so Casey and Sheba would stay put. Mr. Duffy came out, his arms full of bulging shopping bags. They watched him walk slowly over to his car.

"Quick," Annie said. "Let's get the door before it closes."

Mike scooted over and grabbed the door. They ran into the school and straight to Mr. Duffy's office. "Try the door," Annie said. "Maybe he left it unlocked."

Mike turned the knob and leaned against the door. With a low, deep groan, it opened. Mike and Annie stepped into the dark. ❧

CHAPTER 10

A Horrifying Discovery

Mike shut the door and turned on the light.

"What are we looking for?" Annie asked as she surveyed the clutter in the small room.

"I don't know exactly," Mike said. He pointed to the furnace room. "Let's see if we can get in there."

He lifted the latch on the furnace room door and

pushed it open. "What if Mr. Duffy comes back?"
Annie asked.

"We can hide behind the furnace."

"We might get trapped in there."

"Nah, doors always open from inside so people
can get out."

They stepped into a blast of heat. The furnace was
rumbling so much that the room shook. Mike
flicked on the light.

"Look at that," Annie said. She pointed to the shelves along the wall. They were stacked with about thirty containers of every sort—Tupperware, ice cream pails, margarine tubs, lunch kits and pickle jars. Each container was taped shut with a strip of masking tape. There were some words scrawled in felt pen on the tape.

"Hey, there's the lunch kit Mr. Duffy was carrying when Casey lost his bark," Mike said.

"How do you know?"

"It was a Cinderella lunch kit. Why would old Mr. Duffy have a Cinderella lunch kit?"

"Don't know," Annie said. "But come look at this." She pointed to a wooden box at the far end of the shelves.

"What do you think is in this old box?" She picked it up, turned it over and studied the carvings in the wood.

Annie was about to open the box when she stopped dead. There were sounds coming from the outer office. Voices. Getting closer. Mike switched off the light and pulled the door toward him, leaving it open a crack.

They could hear Mr. Duffy and another man in the office arguing. Mr. Duffy said, "I know. I know. But so much trouble. The children...I have to keep them safe."

"What have you done, old man? And what have I done by bringing you here? The news is all over. It won't be long."

Mike recognized that voice. He could tell Annie did too. It was Mr. Mulligan.

"I'm sorry," Mr. Duffy said.

"Can't you stop it?"

"'Tis too late. You saw the crow. Someone is going to die."

"Don't be ridiculous. It's just a crow. But you still need to get them out of here! Get them out of here before the end of the week, before Halloween. They get more restless every day. They're dangerous. Just do it. When I come back tomorrow, I want to see them gone."

Mike and Annie heard the office door slam shut. Mike stood stock-still as a dark shape blocked the light from the partially open door. Mr. Duffy! He was coming into the furnace room.

Mike stepped back, bumping Annie, who dropped the wooden box.

It hit the floor with a loud thump, and the lid popped open.

What happened next was so horrifying that Mike and Annie both screamed at the same time. ❧

CHAPTER 11

The Graveyard Hounds Howl

Mournful, bone chilling, blood curdling howls filled the room and echoed off the walls. It was the sound of big dogs barking, growling and baying like no dogs they had ever heard before—horrible, deep barks and howling-to-the-moon barks. Mike and Annie couldn't hear their own screams over the howling of the baying hounds.

Then Mr. Duffy stepped into the room, slammed the door shut and snapped on the light. He took his pipe out of his pocket, mumbling all the while. He bent down and picked up the box. Holding the box open in one hand, he put the pipe into his mouth with his other hand. He drew on his pipe, and the mournful howling grew softer until it ceased altogether.

Mr. Duffy snapped the lid shut and secured the latch. He placed the box back on the shelf and put the unlit pipe back into his pocket. Then he checked the other containers while Mike and Annie stood frozen in place. When it was all done, he sighed, turned off the light and walked back into his office.

Mike and Annie stood still in the dark room for a moment. They *had* to get out of there, even if they had to face Mr. Duffy. Annie grabbed Mike's sleeve and they stepped softly into the office. Mr. Duffy was filling the teakettle with water. He plugged it in to boil. Then he rummaged around the untidy room, gathering mugs, sugar and milk. When the kettle whistled, it seemed to startle him. He picked it up, poured the boiling water into a large black teapot, put the lid on and set everything on the desk.

Annie and Mike stood waiting for something terrible to happen.

Mr. Duffy pulled two orange kindergarten chairs out from under his desk and signalled for them to sit down.

"Tea?" he asked.

He handed them each a mug. He offered milk, then sugar. He sat down on his chair.

Mike noticed that it swivelled just like Mr. Mulligan's chair. Mr. Duffy swivelled around and took a sip of tea. Then unexpectedly, he put his head down on the desk and sobbed.

Mike and Annie didn't know what to do. Mike concentrated on looking around at the jumbly mess of stuff in the room. Piles of bags and containers lay everywhere. Things were tacked up all over the walls: bits of paper, key chains and rabbits' feet. Mike looked again at Mr. Duffy. The small lumpy figure was still hunched over the desk.

Mr. Duffy sighed heavily and began to mumble. Annie and Mike tried to make sense of what he was saying. It was difficult. After each spurt of words he hiccupped and took a breath. "I tried to help. But accidents happened. Dogs barked. You saw the crow. Now you've heard the Graveyard Hounds. Ahhh. 'Tis bad." He blew his nose loudly and blubbered into his handkerchief.

Mr. Duffy stopped finally and looked at the clock. "'Tis very late," he said. "You should go home now. Your parents will be worried." He walked Mike and Annie outside. He looked around and listened for a moment. The neighbourhood was quiet, buried in fog.

"There's not a dog barking," Mr. Duffy said. "You'll be safe for now. Hurry home. Stop for no one." He stepped back inside the school and pulled the door shut, leaving Mike and Annie alone in the night.

"The dogs," Mike said. "We have to get them."

Casey and Sheba jumped up, wagging their tails as Annie and Mike hurried toward them. They

walked home through the quiet streets. The only noises were familiar sounds: the tire crunch of cars driving down the street, the smack of screen doors slamming, the slap of their footsteps hitting the sidewalk, the soft padding of the dogs beside them.

When they stopped at Annie's apartment, there was a note on the door. Annie read it and said, "My mom's at your place. She wants me to go there."

When Mike opened his door, they were bombarded with questions. "Where have you been?" Mrs. Lee asked.

"Do you kids know what time it is?" Mike's dad asked.

"We were worried," Mike's mom said.

Annie said, "We went to get Casey. He was in the playground. We lost track of the time."

"He's lost his bark too," Mike said.

"Oh, no!" his mom said. She rushed over, stroked Casey's head and rubbed his neck.

"Mike," his dad said, "we need an explanation."

Mike and Annie described what had happened in the playground, the furnace room and Mr. Duffy's office. The room fell silent. Mike waited for his parents to say something, anything, but all he saw was his mom give his dad a weary look. His dad rubbed his chin and looked down at him. Mike knew that the explanation sounded weird. His parents would be disappointed that he hadn't kept an eye on Casey.

"That's what happened," he said in a small voice. Annie nodded in agreement.

"Let's talk about this tomorrow," Mrs. Lee said. "Annie, your dinner's waiting." She took Annie's arm and they went home.

Mike turned to his mom and dad. "You believe me, don't you?" he asked.

He waited. He could tell that they were wondering if this was just another of his excuses, only this time a really wacky one.

His father thought for a moment. "Mike," he said, "I do believe that something happened. But there's usually a reason for things, and imagination can play tricks on you."

"But Mr. Duffy was there when Casey lost his bark."

"Just coincidence."

"We heard the barking in the furnace room."

"You dropped a wooden box and it made a sound. Then you probably heard rumbling sounds from the furnace. Old furnaces can be really noisy, especially when they're working overtime on a cold day," his dad said.

"But what about all the strange stuff Mr. Duffy told us?"

"Warnings from a cantankerous old man trying to keep kids out of the school at night. School custodians can seem a little odd sometimes."

"But we heard Mr. Mulligan."

"He's the *principal*."

Mike stopped trying to explain. He looked down at the floor. Casey stood beside him, looking down too.

"I'll talk to the vet tomorrow, Mike," his mom said gently.

"I'll see what I can find out too," his dad said. "Maybe this has happened somewhere else. Someone might have written about it." ❧

CHAPTER 12

Be Careful What You Say

When Mike came home from school the next day, he was full of curiosity and hope. Maybe his dad had learned something. Maybe, just maybe, his mom had some good news from the vet.

Mike opened the door to his apartment, his head full of questions. But someone else was already there doing the asking.

"Come and sit down, Mike," his mom said. "We're being interviewed." Mike looked over to the other side of the room, expecting to see the reporter they saw on the news each night. But it wasn't him. Mike did recognize the man, however. It was the stranger from the playground.

"He's here to ask about Casey," his mom explained.

Mike couldn't see Casey anywhere.

The man from the Unnatural News Network was sitting on a chair across from Mike's mom. He smiled at Mike.

Mike knew he had to sit down. Suddenly, he didn't feel very well. He walked over to sit beside his mom and took a long look at the stranger. The man still had his coat on. It was a shiny black raincoat. It reminded Mike of wet feathers.

Mike couldn't stop staring as the man kept chatting with his mother. The man was smiling oddly even as he talked. And the way he leaned down when he spoke was weird, like a bird pecking at something. It made his nose look like a beak. Mike knew that there was something about this man that was very dangerous. He had felt it in the playground, and he felt it now. How could his mom sit there and smile at this stranger?

And where was Casey? Why hadn't he come to meet him at the door? "How's Casey, Mom?" Mike asked at last. "Did his bark come back?"

"No, no. And Casey won't come out of your room. Why don't you see if you can bring him out?"

Mike got up and walked slowly so that no one would see he was feeling unsteady. He felt better as soon as he entered his room. He saw Casey under the bed. "Casey," he called softly. "Come here."

The dog's nose poked out. Mike could hear the tiny thumps of his tail hitting the floor, but the dog

refused to move. Mike crouched down. Casey looked gloomy like only a dog can. "Come out, Casey," Mike said. But Casey wouldn't budge. Mike patted the trembling dog. "Are you okay, boy?" Casey thumped his tail in response, looked at Mike with his sad black eyes, but kept his head down.

Mike didn't want to go back into the living room, but he knew if he didn't they would come looking for him. He did not want that stranger anywhere near his room or his dog. "Stay here, boy," he said, and walked out into the living room.

His mom was still talking to the reporter. "Yes," she said. "Both dogs are affected. Sheba, the sheltie, doesn't seem to have lost her good nature, though. And Casey was in good spirits last night when he came home. But today he doesn't seem like his usual self."

The stranger was nodding and looking at Mike's mom.

Mike sat down again and tried to keep his hands from shaking.

"Indeed, that is strange," said the man. "And you say these dogs seem to have both lost their barks on the school grounds? Was there anyone else around? A witness, someone I could talk to?" He opened his notepad. He turned to Mike and smiled that horrible smile.

Mike hesitated, feeling uneasy.

"Mike," his mom said, "tell the reporter who was with you."

"Only Annie," Mike said.

"Annie? Your friend from the playground?" asked the man.

"Yeah."

"I spoke to her mother on Sunday. Is she the only one?"

"Yeah."

"We have their story. But we are looking for others who might know something. The principal of the school perhaps? Was he there when your dogs lost their barks?"

"Mr. Mulligan?" Mike got the strangest feeling that the stranger knew the answer and was trying to trick him just like Mr. Mulligan had in his office. You had to watch what you said. "No, he wasn't there," he said.

"Tell me about the principal. Does he like dogs?"

"I guess so," Mike said.

"He lets kids bring dogs to school?"

"No. He doesn't like us doing that."

"Most interesting. Perhaps there is a reason for that rule." The man smiled again.

Mike didn't answer. He was thinking about Mr. Mulligan. How was he mixed up in all of this?

Mike could feel the stranger's eyes on him.

"You're sure there was no one else around?" the man asked. "Surely there are others who work at the school who might know something about this."

"You said you saw Mr. Duffy there, Mike," his mom said. "He might know something."

The man jerked his head toward Mike's mom. "This Mr. Duffy, who is he? Does he work there?" He made a note on his pad.

"Yes," Mike's mom said.

"What does he do?"

"Why, he's the custodian. He looks after the school," she said.

"A custodian. Like a caretaker?"

Mike was feeling sick again. The man was asking too many questions. Why was he so interested in Mr. Duffy?

"Has this Mr. Duffy been the caretaker for a long time?"

"I don't know," Mike's mom said. "Has he?" She looked over at Mike.

"No," Mike replied.

"How long?" the reporter asked.

"I don't know. Not long."

"Was he there at the school when dogs started to lose their barks?" the reporter asked.

"I'm not sure," Mike lied. He didn't trust this man at all.

Mr. Corone snapped his notepad shut and looked at Mike. "I'll have to speak to Mr. Duffy myself. Would he be at the school now?"

Mike wanted to stop this man from going to the school. "Maybe," he said. "But no one can get in. It's all locked up now."

"But he'll be there tomorrow?"

"Maybe."

The reporter put his pen and notebook into his pocket and smiled. He stood up and swooped toward the door.

"Will this story be on the news?" Mike's mom asked. "Will *we* be on the news?"

But the man had already flown out the door.

No one said anything for a moment. Casey trotted out from the bedroom. Mike called him over and hugged him.

"Casey's probably just gloomy about losing his bark," Mike's mom said. "I did talk to the vet today, and she's puzzled by it. But he's a healthy dog. Nothing else is wrong with him. Your dad will be home soon. We'll see if he knows anything else."

Somehow, Mike didn't think that his dad could have come up with anything. His father was always looking for a reasonable explanation for things. Mike suspected the explanation might be strange, maybe even unnatural, like that reporter said.

He had to talk to Annie. 🐾

CHAPTER 13

A Close Call

Mike told Annie about the reporter's visit.

"Hmmm," Annie said. "I think we should tell Mr. Duffy about this."

"Yeah. But what about Mr. Mulligan?" Mike asked.

Annie shook her head. "I'm not sure about him yet."

"Okay," Mike said. "But we should tell Mr. Duffy right now. My dad will be home soon. He might come looking for me at your place."

They ran to the school.

They spotted Mr. Duffy beside the tree that had been struck by lightning. He was huddled over, holding a pail in one hand and poking at something on the ground. When they got closer, they saw that it was a dead squirrel.

Mr. Duffy sighed. He pointed to the squirrel and held out the pail for them to see the firecrackers and matches inside. "Crow on the tree. Dead squirrel on the ground," he said. "And fire. Ahhh, 'tis bad."

He looked directly at Annie and Mike. "Did you hear any dogs barking after school today?" he asked.

"No," they both said at once.

"Then why has this happened?" Mr. Duffy picked up the squirrel with a pair of tongs and placed it gently into the pail.

Mike was about to ask Mr. Duffy what he was talking about, but he stopped suddenly. There was a loud cracking sound.

"Look out!" a voice cried out. "Look out! Above you!"

Mike looked up. The big branch was falling, finally breaking away from the tree and the fence. It was directly above Annie.

Just as suddenly, she was pushed aside. The branch crashed harmlessly to the ground.

"Are you hurt, Annie?" It was Mr. Mulligan. "I'm sorry I had to push you," he said, holding out his hand to help her up.

"I'm okay," Annie said. "Thank you."

Mike could see that she wasn't hurt, but she looked scared.

"I'll take you home," Mr. Mulligan said.

"No," Annie said. "I'm fine." She took a little package out of her pocket. "My lucky stars," she whispered to Mike.

"Please, Annie, come inside," said Mr. Mulligan. "We'll call your mother."

"She won't be home for another half hour," Annie said.

"Oh," said Mr. Mulligan. "Well, please go right home. Tell your mom to give me a call." Mr. Mulligan turned around and walked back toward the school.

Mr. Duffy shuffled off slowly, picking up Halloween debris and muttering to himself.

"Mr. Duffy!" Mike called.

Mr. Duffy turned toward them and waited. "What is it you're wanting?"

"Someone is looking for you, Mr. Duffy," Mike said.

"Looking for me?" He looked at them warily. "Now who would be looking for me?"

"He says he's a reporter—from the Unnatural News Network. He asked about you."

Mr. Duffy put the pail and tongs on the ground. "And what is it he was asking?"

Mike hesitated. "He asked about the dogs, about them losing their barks."

"Ah, but everyone's been asking about that. Isn't it in the news now?"

"This man said his name was Mr. Corone. He asked how long you had worked here." Mike saw Mr. Duffy shudder at the sound of the name.

"He has come then," Mr. Duffy said, his eyes full of fear. "I am found. 'Tis over for me."

Annie said gently, "Why is he here, Mr. Duffy? Why is he looking for you?"

Mr. Duffy didn't answer.

"Is it about the dogs?" Annie asked.

Mr. Duffy looked down and put his head in his hands. "Yes. 'Tis about the dogs."

"Mr. Duffy, you helped us. We want to help you," Mike said.

"There's no one can help me," he said.

"Mr. Duffy, tell us about the dogs," Mike said.

"I cannot do that."

"Why was Mr. Corone asking about our dogs?" Mike asked.

"Them's not the dogs he's coming after," Mr. Duffy said.

"What dogs is he after then?" Annie asked.

"The Graveyard Hounds."

"The Graveyard Hounds? What are they?" Mike asked.

"'Tis a terrible, terrible story I have to tell you. But I cannot tell you here," Mr. Duffy said. "Come with me to my office."

CHAPTER 14

The Curse of the Graveyard Hounds

IRELAND, MY VILLAGE

Even before they all sat down, Mr. Duffy started to mumble. Eventually the mumbling became a story. It was a story so bizarre that both Annie and Mike knew it had to be true. For who could make up such a tale?

"I was a caretaker in Ireland too," Mr. Duffy said. "But not in a school full of children. I cared for the village graveyard. At night I would hear the Graveyard Hounds howling, the Hounds of Cuchulain."

"Who?" Annie asked.

"Cuchulain, the great warrior. He was killed in battle a long, long time ago. Such a great hero he was. His enemies were so afraid of him that even when he died in his last battle, they would not believe it or go near his body until they saw a black bird light on his shoulder. That was the proof that he was truly dead. He was buried on a mound. His faithful dogs would not leave his graveside."

"His dogs?" Mike asked.

"Yes. Great wolfhounds they were. Then down through the centuries, people said, the dogs roamed the countryside by day and howled on the mound by night. The Hounds of Cuchulain, people said. When the Hounds howled 'twas a sign that someone would die. So many graves grew up around the mound. Then something happened."

"What happened?" Annie asked.

"The supervisor of the graveyard keepers discovered an ancient magic, a spell in an old pipe that could capture the howling of the Hounds. He used the magic to get the howling and put it into a wooden box."

"Why?" Mike asked.

"To control the people in the village and to steal what little they had. When he walked through the streets carrying the box, everyone hurried away, barred the windows and locked the doors, desperate to keep him out. How I dreaded the howling of the Graveyard Hounds. It was unbearable. I had to do something to stop it."

"What did you do?" Annie asked.

"I stole the magic pipe," Mr. Duffy said. He looked at the furnace room door. "But worse, I stole the Graveyard Hounds."

"You stole the Hounds?" Mike asked.

"Not the Hounds themselves, mind you," Mr. Duffy said. "I stole the howls. You heard them that day in the furnace room."

"The Graveyard Hounds are *here*?" Annie asked.

"Yes. I took their howls and came to this town to hide. But I had to get work. It was hard because

people said I was too old.
Mr. Mulligan helped.
We know each other.
He came from the
same village. I helped
his family when he was
a boy. I protected them from

the Hounds. He got me a job as the school custodian.
I work hard, but I have only brought trouble. So
many accidents—the fire, Annie's hand, the crow
and the dead squirrel. Annie was almost killed just
now. And there's worse to come yet, 'tis certain."

"But what about our dogs?" Mike asked.

"Your dogs?" Mr. Duffy asked.

"Yes. Sheba and Casey. We saw you at the adventure
playground when they lost their barks. Do you know
what happened to them?" Annie asked.

"Ahhh. Yes."

"Did you take their barks?" Mike asked.

"Yes."

"But why? They're not dangerous," Annie said.

"I was trying to help," he said.

"Help? How?" Mike asked.

"The Graveyard Hounds have ancient powers. They are not of this earth. They can hear your dogs on the playground. Dogs' hearing is so much better than people's, you know. When your dogs bark, the Hounds take strength from it and become even stronger. So I had to stop your dogs from barking. Especially now, just before Halloween. 'Tis when the Hounds become more and more restless. Bad things happen. I had to steal the barks from your dogs."

"But how did you do it?" Mike asked.

"With this." Mr. Duffy held up his pipe, turned it over in his hands and looked at the kids sitting there. "This holds the magic." He sighed heavily. "It draws the barking of a dog into an empty container. 'Tis so easy."

"Where are the barks for Sheba and Casey?" Annie asked.

Mr. Duffy got up and went into the furnace room. Mike heard him rummaging around and muttering. He came out carrying the Cinderella lunch kit. On a strip of masking tape were the words "Maybe a Lab. Large."

Mr. Duffy put the lunch kit on his desk and shuffled back into the furnace room. He came back holding a Tupperware container. It was labelled "Black and white sheltie. Medium." Mr. Duffy put it next to the lunch kit.

"Your dogs' barks are in there," he said.

They all sat quietly for a minute. Mike studied the Cinderella lunch kit that Mr. Duffy said had Casey's bark in it. He looked at the shopping bags and containers piled around the room and remembered the ones stacked on the shelves in the furnace room. Dog barks stuffed in containers. *The old guy is really crazy,* thought Mike. He looked at Mr. Duffy slumped down in the chair.

"Can you give the dogs their barks back?" Mike asked.

"No. 'Twould be impossible," Mr. Duffy said.

"Why?" Annie asked.

"They belong to the Hounds now," Mr. Duffy said.

"Why did you bring the Graveyard Hounds to school?" Mike asked.

"To keep everyone safe and sound, I must keep them with me. The Hounds sleep during the day, so I put them here in the furnace room. It has a big thick door, and the furnace is loud and grumbly. 'Tis easy to hide the growling sounds when they get restless. I take them home at night and lock them away."

"Do all the containers in the furnace room have dog barks in them?" Annie asked.

"Yes," Mr. Duffy said. "But 'tis all over now. Corvus Corone has found me."

"That reporter," Annie said.

"He's no reporter." Mr. Duffy wrung his hands. "He's the man I stole the Hounds from."

"Who is he really?" Mike asked

"He's the supervisor of the graveyard keepers. He comes from a long line of them. That's the man that'll come and take everything—the howls and the pipe. Without them, he has no power." Mr. Duffy looked at Annie sadly. "But there is more."

"What?" Mike asked.

"You and Annie have heard the howling. And wasn't Annie almost killed today? Everyone here is in terrible danger, I tell you. Look at the dead squirrel, the crow and the fire. 'Tis obvious. These are signs. Someone will die before the week is out."

The room trembled. The furnace rumbled and the clock ticked, but there was another sound.

It was the sound of the door opening. ❧

CHAPTER 15

A Hopeless Situation

"Mike. Annie. What are you two doing here?"

It was Mr. Mulligan. He stood in the doorway looking down at them over the top of his glasses.

"They know," Mr. Duffy said.

"Oh," Mr. Mulligan said. "Oh dear!"

Mr. Mulligan came into the room, pulled out a kindergarten chair and sat down. He looked odd sitting on it facing them as if *he* were a kid called to the principal's office.

Mike stood up and looked down at Mr. Mulligan. "We heard you talking in Mr. Duffy's office," he said. "You told Mr. Duffy to get rid of something by Halloween."

Mr. Mulligan didn't say anything.

"Was it the Graveyard Hounds?" Annie asked.

"Yes," Mr. Mulligan said. "But that is not quite what I said he must do."

"What did you say, Mr. Mulligan?" Mike asked.

"I said to get them out of here, out of the school. Getting rid of them is another matter entirely."

"How *do* you get rid of them?" Annie asked.

"There is only one way. And it is dangerous," Mr. Mulligan said.

"Tell them," said Mr. Duffy.

"I can explain it much better in my office," said Mr. Mulligan. "Follow me."

They moved silently through the dark school. Annie and Mike walked behind Mr. Duffy and Mr. Mulligan.

Mr. Mulligan went into his office and turned on the desk lamp. They followed him inside, standing with Mr. Duffy in the half-light as he searched the bookshelves. Finally, Mr. Mulligan pulled out a very old, thin, brown leather book and placed it on his desk. He motioned for Mike and Annie to sit down.

"This terrible trouble will all end tomorrow

night," Mr. Mulligan said. He sat down himself and adjusted his glasses. "Listen." He began to read aloud from the book. "Only on the night of the Great Feast of Samhain, can the Hounds of Cuchulain be reunited with the Great Warrior in the Realm of the Dead."

Mr. Mulligan looked up and said, "The night of the Great Feast of Samhain—*that's tomorrow night.*"

Annie and Mike looked at each other.

Halloween, Mike thought.

Mr. Mulligan continued reading: "Their journey is through fire. Only then can the restless souls of

the Graveyard Hounds find peace and cease their unearthly howling as harbingers of death."

"Go on," Mr. Duffy said. "Read where it tells who must do this."

Mr. Mulligan turned a few pages and continued to read. "Those who accompany the Hounds, to send them on their journey, must be brave beyond measure and noble of spirit—brave to venture into the realm of the dead and noble to risk their lives for others."

"Tell them why it is so dangerous," Mr. Duffy said.

Mr. Mulligan read: "They must be gone from the graveyard by midnight—before the last Graveyard Hound stops howling—or forever wander the land between the living and the dead. To fail is to be forever doomed."

He closed the book.

Mr. Duffy mumbled, "I cannot do any more. My bravery, 'tis all used up. 'Tis hopeless."

"It was brave you were, old man, to steal the Hounds," said Mr. Mulligan. "But look what you've done by bringing them here!"

"But who will do it?" said Mr. Duffy.

"I will," Mr. Mulligan said solemnly as he turned to look at Mike and Annie.

Mr. Mulligan walked Mr. Duffy to the door. "You've done enough, old man."

Mike glanced at the book on Mr. Mulligan's desk, grabbed it and slipped it inside his coat. Annie looked at him, her eyes wide with surprise.

"Time to go home," Mr. Mulligan said, switching off the light.

ᵞᵧ

On the way home, Annie said, "It's impossible. How can anyone outrun a howl?"

"I don't know," Mike said.

"Brave and noble. And fast," said Annie. "What about Mr. Mulligan? Can he do this?"

"He said he would. But I dunno. He's even afraid of grandmas. He'd probably be afraid of this. I think he can run, though."

"Could your dad do this?" Annie asked.

Mike thought for a minute. "No," he said. "My dad doesn't believe in this kind of stuff."

"What about Ritchie?" Annie asked. "He could do it."

"Maybe," Mike said. "We could ask him."

In the light of the stairwell, Mike opened the book and flipped through the pages. He stopped at a page with a picture of a gigantic warrior holding a sword. Two massive dogs stood by his side.

"Look at this," he said, holding out the book for Annie to see. "That must be Cuchulain and his dogs."

Mike read: "Only on this one night can the curse be lifted. If the Howls are consumed by fire, the curse will end."

Annie reached out to take the book. She studied the picture and the words underneath. Then she tapped her fingers on the page. "Look at this! It says the fire sets the Hounds free."

ᵞ ᵧ

That night, Mike couldn't stop thinking about the book. He dreamt he was running through a graveyard with a pack of dogs chasing after him. They were phantom dogs whose ghostly wails hounded him until he fell, tumbling down into a bottomless grave.

Mike woke up gasping for air. He felt Casey's nose nudge him in the dark. Mike brought the big dog onto the bed and fell back to sleep.

When he woke up next morning, he heard a scratching at the window. He pulled open the curtains to see a single crow clawing at the window ledge. Mr. Duffy's words came back to him: *A crow on the thatch, soon death lifts the latch.*

Someone was going to die.

But who? ❧

CHAPTER 16

Halloween Day

Mike and Annie were surprised to see the playground full of ghosts and goblins of every size and sort.

"We forgot to wear our Halloween costumes," Mike said.

"I didn't feel like it anyway," Annie said.

Just after the bell, Mike was called to the principal's office.

He knows I stole the book, he thought. *Big trouble.* No excuses were going to help him. *Suspension for sure.*

Mrs. Williams didn't make him wait this time. That was another sign of trouble. "Go right in, Mike," she said.

Mike opened the door to face Mr. Mulligan, who was standing in front of his desk. Mr. Mulligan was wearing the same Halloween costume he wore every year—a detective's raincoat and hat, a big nose and glasses and a fake moustache. He stared at Mike over the top of the goofy glasses.

"Where is the book?" Mr. Mulligan asked.

"It's right here," Mike said, pulling it out of his

jacket. "I was bringing it back."

"Now Mike," Mr. Mulligan said. "This is a very dangerous business. It is not a job for a boy."

"But the dogs...and the crow!" Mike protested.

The phone rang. Mr. Mulligan picked it up. He looked at Mike as he listened. His face, the part that Mike could see, went white. "Yes. I'll tell him," he said, hanging up. Mr. Mulligan sat down on the desk. "Mike, that was your mom. She wants me to tell you that your brother has been in an accident. On the way to school, he was hit by a car. Your mom and dad are with him at the hospital."

Mike thought about the crow on the window. Was Ritchie going to die?

"The doctors say Ritchie's going to be okay," Mr. Mulligan said. "Your dad will pick you up after school."

ᗉᖶ

Mr. Mulligan walked Mike back to class, past the posters of rules and violations. "I'm sure Ritchie will be fine," he said. "I'll let you know if I get any more information." When they stopped at the classroom door, he added, "I have work to do now, Mike. The Hounds need looking after."

Mike watched the principal stride away in his slouchy raincoat. *I hope you can do it, Mr. Mulligan,* he thought.

Mike walked into the class, his head pounding. *Someone will die. The Hounds…harbingers of death… the curse…consumed by fire…*

ᗉᖶ

"I'm sure Ritchie's accident was no accident," Mike said to Annie at recess.

"I'll bet that reporter Corone had something to do with it," Annie said.

"First you and now Ritchie," Mike said. "Who'll be next?"

"I think Corone will come for Mr. Duffy, don't you?"

Mike nodded.

"He'll come to get the Hounds," Annie said. "Corone must know that if someone is going to free the Hounds, it has to be tonight."

"You're right," Mike said. "He'll come to the school before midnight to get the Hounds. We have to watch out for him."

↟↟

At noon they hung around the basement. They didn't see Mr. Duffy, but once or twice they thought they heard the Hounds growl.

They're still in there, Mike thought.

The afternoon stretched out like a strange dream. Miss Walters lit the jack-o'-lanterns; they played games and listened to ghost stories.

I'm in a ghost story, Mike thought, *and I don't know how it will end.* He worried about Ritchie. What if he wasn't all right? Mike couldn't wait to see his dad, to ask him about Ritchie. He thought the three o'clock bell would never ring.

But his dad wasn't there to meet him. ❖

CHAPTER 17

The Beginning of the End

"Something's wrong," Mike said.

"Let's check the office," Annie said. "Maybe your dad called the school."

Mrs. Williams was hanging up the telephone. "I was just talking to your dad," she said. "He's still at the hospital with your brother. Your mom's there too. You're to go home with Annie."

"We don't have to hurry home," Annie said to Mike. "Let's go down to the basement and check out Mr. Duffy's office."

The basement was dark and deserted. Mr. Duffy's office door was closed. Mike knocked, but he didn't wait for an answer this time. He turned the knob and pushed slowly. The door creaked a bit as it opened. The first thing Mike saw was that the furnace room

door was open. The
furnace was making
its grumbling noises,
but there were no other
sounds. Annie whispered,
"You watch for Mr. Duffy.
I'll look for the Hounds."

Mike squinted into the darkness and
listened for footsteps. He could hear Annie moving
around in the furnace room.

"The Hounds are gone!" Annie said. "Corone must
have been here. The room's a mess. But I have Sheba
and Casey's barks." She held up the Cinderella
lunchbox and the Tupperware container.

Suddenly, Mike heard voices.

"Shhh!" Mike whispered to her. "Stay there." He
listened for a moment. "It's him. Corone. And he's
arguing with Mr. Mulligan. They're coming closer."
Mike moved away from the door.

"Quick!" Annie whispered. "Into the furnace room."

Annie switched off the light just in time. They
could see Mr. Mulligan stumbling into Mr. Duffy's
office. Corone was pushing him.

"He's not here. He's gone," Mr. Mulligan said. "You're too late."

"I've already been to see Duffy, that old fool. I've got the pipe. He doesn't have the Hounds. They're still in the school. I know! I've been watching all day. You've got them. Tell me where they are!"

Corone poked and pushed at Mr. Mulligan with his claw-like hands. They scuffled. Mr. Mulligan fell against the desk. He struggled to stand and grabbed Corone by the arm. Annie and Mike stared in horror as Corone pushed him again and they both fell to the floor. Mr. Mulligan lay still, moaning. Corone stood up, hopped around a bit, straightened his coat and looked down at Mr. Mulligan.

"I know where the Hounds will be at midnight," Corone said as he swooped out. Mike and Annie heard him walk away, banging the exit door shut behind him.

"Mr. Mulligan's hurt," Mike said.

They hurried out of the furnace room and knelt beside him. Mr. Mulligan pulled himself up. His glasses were broken and he was bleeding from a cut on the back of his head.

"Help me get up the stairs," he said.

At the top of the stairs, he stopped and said, "I can get myself to the office now. Mrs. Williams will call for help. You go home."

✶✶

"Let's not go outside yet," Annie said. "Corone might still be out there."

Annie and Mike sat down on the basement steps. Night was approaching. It was becoming even darker in the school basement. They could hardly see anything—only dark shadows and the red lights from the signs above the exit doors. They sat very still, listening, while outside firecrackers popped, and inside the furnace rumbled and the old building creaked its weary old sounds. It was spooky.

The sound of a siren startled them. It was close. It came closer. They heard tires crunching the gravel on the school grounds.

"An ambulance," Annie said. "It must be here for Mr. Mulligan."

Mike sat slumped in worry. Poor Mr. Mulligan.

It got quiet again.

"Ritchie and now Mr. Mulligan," Annie said. "Who will take the Hounds to the graveyard now?"

Mike knew what Annie was thinking.

"It will have to be us," he said.

"Yes."

"We'll have to get the Hounds," he said. "They're still here in the school."

"How will we find them?"

"Mr. Duffy said they get restless at Halloween," Mike said. "We can listen for them. They'll be growling." 🐾

CHAPTER 18

Secret Hiding Places

Mike and Annie stood up and began walking.

"Do you think anyone else is still around?" Mike asked.

"The night custodian. It won't be Mr. Duffy," Annie said. "We have to be careful."

They began walking down the halls, first one side and then the other, their ears close to the walls. They heard lots of sounds—sounds they never heard during the day—the scritching and scratching of mice and lost hamsters, the slap of tree branches against the windows and the rumbly sigh of the furnace as it turned itself on and off. But they didn't hear the growling of the Hounds.

Mike tried to organize the jumble of thoughts in his head. Was Ritchie going to die?

When they reached the third floor of the school, they knew it was their last hope. There was nowhere else to look for the Hounds. At the top of the stairwell outside the music room, Mike thought he heard something. The noise was soft, barely audible, a low growl.

"Listen," he said.

They stood still and held their breath. Yes, it was a growl, and it seemed to be coming from above the ceiling.

Mike looked up. He saw a flicker of light. The trap door to the attic had been moved. "Looks like someone's been up there and left in a hurry," he whispered.

"The Hounds must be up there," Annie said.

"Keep watch down here. I'm going up," Mike said.

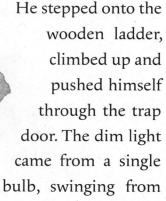

He stepped onto the wooden ladder, climbed up and pushed himself through the trap door. The dim light came from a single bulb, swinging from above. There was stuff everywhere—old furniture, books, boxes and shelves. Everything was covered in cobwebs and thick dust.

Mike listened intently. The Hounds had stopped their growling. *If the Hounds don't growl, I'll never find them in here*, he thought.

He stood very still, waiting for the growls to start again. And they did—low muffled woofs and deep menacing growls. It made Mike's skin crawl. He looked around, trying to locate the box in the giant heap of clutter. As the light flickered, he caught a glimpse of something on the floor in front of an old armchair. The dust had been scraped away. And there was the box, underneath the chair. Mike grabbed it and hurried down the ladder.

"The Hounds are waking up," he said to Annie. He put the box under his jacket. "Come on. Let's get out of here quick."

"Do you think Corone is outside?" Annie asked.

"No," Mike said. "He doesn't know anyone's here now. I think he'll come for them at midnight."

As they hurried home, the fog closed in around them.

They went directly to Annie's, got the key for her storage locker and went down to the basement of the apartment building. They placed the box under a shelf. "Corone doesn't know where I live," Annie said. "The Hounds are safe here for now."

"I think we should leave Sheba and Casey's barks here too," Mike said.

⅄⅄

Annie's mom was home when they got back to the apartment. She had Casey with her.

"Your mom and dad are still at the hospital, Mike," she said. "You can stay here overnight. I'll make up a bed for you in the spare room. Do you want to go trick-or-treating or stay home and watch a movie?"

"We'll watch a movie," Annie said.

🐾

"It's late," Annie's mom said when the movie ended. "Time to call it a night. Lights out, you two. I'm taking the dogs outside now for their walk." They watched as she headed off with Casey and Sheba down the hallway to the stairs. Then Annie closed the door.

"Check the clock," she said.

No time to waste. 🐾

CHAPTER 19

Freeing the Restless Souls

"Listen," Annie said. "I hear knocking in the hall."

They peeked out into the hallway. A man was knocking on Mike's apartment door. They closed the door quietly.

Mike whispered, "Corone. He's out there."

"He's come to get the Hounds," Annie said.

"Shhh," Mike said. "Footsteps."

They heard the footsteps walking down the hall. They heard the hum of the elevator, and then it was quiet again.

Without a word, they got ready. They emptied out their backpacks. Annie gathered matches and a pile of newspapers. She stuffed everything into her backpack. Then she got a shopping bag. "To carry Casey and Sheba's barks," she explained, handing it to Mike. They put on their coats. Annie checked her pocket to make sure she had her lucky stars and put the locker room key into her pocket too.

Mike checked the time again. Only minutes until midnight.

They opened the door slowly and ran through the hall and down the stairs. As they stepped out of the stairwell into the basement, they heard party sounds. Music. Voices. Laughter. They hurried the other way. Annie got out the key and opened the door to the storage lockers.

Annie put the Tupperware container and the Cinderella lunchbox into the shopping bag while Mike reached under the shelf for the Hounds. He held the box carefully, making sure the latch was snapped on tightly. He could hear soft growling as he put the box into his coat.

Mike spotted some broken pieces of an old wooden chair. "We'll need this for the fire," he explained, as he stuffed the wood into his backpack.

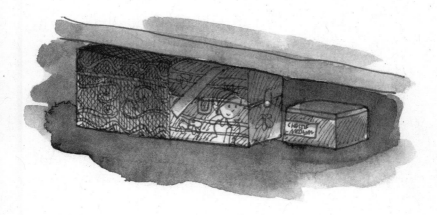

Annie opened the door to the hallway and looked out. "All clear," she said. They ran up to the lobby and outside into the gloomy night.

When they reached the graveyard gates, Annie and Mike heard the sound of footsteps behind them. They turned around. The footsteps stopped. All they could see was the swirling fog.

Annie gripped the shopping bag, and Mike clutched the wooden box. He looked at Annie. She nodded. They passed between the blackened gateposts into the graveyard. As they made their way, they tripped over roots and bumped against gravestones. Then they stumbled upon a mound of freshly dug earth. Beside it, there was an open grave.

"Cuchulain was buried on a mound," Annie said.

"Then let's make the fire here," Mike said.

They put the box and the shopping bag on the ground and went to work. They did not speak. They dared not make any noise.

They emptied their backpacks, setting the match-box, newspapers and wood on the ground. Mike crumpled some newspapers and placed them in a pile on the mound, close to the open grave. Annie put some sticks of wood on top. Shaking, Mike struck a match. It did not light.

He opened the matchbox to get another. It was so cold that his fingers wouldn't work properly. The matches tumbled out of the box and fell to the ground. Mike bent down to pick them up before they got wet.

He could feel the power of the Graveyard Hounds growing. The wooden box was tumbling around in the fog and the earth was shaking. Annie grabbed the box. "Hurry," she said. "I don't know how long I can hold them in. They're stronger now."

Mike tried to light another match, slowly this time, cupping his hand against the cold. It lit up. He placed the burning match onto the pile of newspapers and threw on more matches. The fire sizzled and smoked in the damp air and went out.

Mike lit the last match. Trembling, he held the flame to a dry corner of the newspaper. The paper burst into flame and the fire took hold. Mike put the rest of the newspaper and wood on the fire and stood back. He felt the distant earth tremble. Someone or something was approaching.

The fire flared up into the darkness. Annie handed
him the wooden box and moved away from the fire.
The Hounds were growling so fiercely now that it
seemed the box would explode. Mike's hands felt
numb.

"Help!" he heard Annie call. "Mike! Help!"

Mike looked up, horrified. Corone was holding
Annie. His long nails, like
talons, dug into her
shoulder.

"The box," he said.
"Give it to me. Or she
goes into the
fire." Corone
pushed Annie
toward the
flames.

The fire was
roaring now.
Annie's frightened
face looked
at Mike.
Corone was

tapping his fingers on her shoulder, his nails gleaming in the firelight.

"The box," Corone said again. "Give it to me." He pushed Annie right to the edge of the fire. Annie's little packet of lucky stars fell into the grave. Mike felt the wooden box in his hand. He had to think. Would Corone let go of Annie if he handed over the box? How could he be sure?

Then Mike caught a glimpse of something moving in the fog behind Annie and Corone. Two huge shapes burst out of the night into the firelight. They leaped at Corone. It was Casey and Sheba! At that moment, Annie broke free from Corone's grasp and Mike yelled, "Here is the box!" He threw it into the flames.

Corone darted forward, reaching into the fire to grab the box. But he was too late. As the box crackled and burned, the howling of the great Hounds shattered the air. The fire exploded into a raging inferno. Burning fangs seized Corone. As he scrambled to get away, black feathers flew up from his coat. Then down, down he tumbled, into the dark grave. The Hounds howled ferociously.

Annie came to stand beside Mike. Casey and Sheba stood close by. On the mound, the flaming figure of a Celtic warrior, wielding a huge battle sword and shield, rose up from the fire. The mighty warrior towered above the two children and their dogs. All the while, the Hounds howled.

"Cuchulain!" Mike said in awe. Annie nodded, hardly able to hear over the din of the Hounds.

Cuchulain, the hero from long ago, placed his sword in its scabbard and opened his arms. Two enormous dogs emerged from the depths of the fire. Cuchulain spoke some strange words and the Hounds rushed toward him. He gathered their fiery bodies into his cloak and closed it around them. At last, the Graveyard Hounds were free.

Then Cuchulain stared down into the grave. Mike and Annie looked down too. They saw a black bird fly up, dripping fire and feathers. The bird came to rest on Cuchulain's shoulder.

The midnight bells rang out. Mike could see that the fire was dying, turning in on itself. Suddenly, he remembered the warning in the prophecy.

"We have to get out of here *now*!" Mike yelled. "Before the Hounds stop howling!"

The cemetery was still buried in deep fog. How would they find their way out in time? Mike grabbed Casey by the collar. "Home, Casey," he shouted. "Run, Annie! Casey, Sheba. Run!"

The dogs ran. Annie and Mike, hearts pounding, ran close beside them. They could hear the Hounds howl. Just as they tumbled through the blackened gateposts, the howling stopped.

The midnight bells fell silent and the fog was swept away.

Annie and Mike looked up to see Annie's mom.

"Mom! What are *you* doing here?" Annie asked.

"The dogs took off when I unleashed them. They must have come looking for you. It's midnight! Why are *you* here?"

Just then Sheba and Casey started to bark excitedly.

"Sheba! Casey! You've got your barks back!" Mike said.

And the streets echoed with joyful barking. 🐾

On the news the next morning, the reporter said, "There was another fire in the graveyard last night. Halloween and fire and graveyards seem to go together. And that story we've been following about dogs losing their barks? Well, folks, it's still a mystery. We can't explain it, but it seems our dogs have got their barks back.

"We turn our attention now to a serious incident that happened at the local school. It has been reported that the principal, Mr. Mulligan, was injured in an altercation with an intruder. He was taken to hospital. Police are investigating."

Mike was sure that Ritchie and Mr. Mulligan would be all right. When his dad said, "Ritchie is out of danger. He wants to see you," Mike was not surprised. He could hardly wait to see his brother. And he could hardly wait to see Mr. Mulligan. "You have quite a story to tell them," Mike's dad said.

\vspace{4pt}

After school, Mike and Annie took Casey and Sheba to the playground before going to the hospital. It was a sunny day, the first one since the dogs had lost their barks. While Casey and Sheba ran around, Mike and Annie scanned the school building to see if anyone was looking out.

A movement at one of the windows high above caught Mike's eye. "Annie," Mike said, "look there— at that window! Something's moving."

Annie looked up. "Where?" she asked.

"There," he said, pointing. "I think it's Mr. Duffy."

They stared for a long time at the windows. Mike was sure he had seen someone. But as the sun set and dusk fell, the windows grew dark.

Whoever it was had disappeared. ❖

ACKNOWLEDGEMENTS

Every writer must have a friend who will read a work in progress with a critical and helpful eye. Finola Finlay is my literary friend. For this book, she was also a source of information, being Irish and having knowledge about Cuchulain in Irish literature. Thank you. I am also thankful to Michael Kaufman-Lacusta for his editorial work. I appreciated his comments and suggestions during the long time that it took to complete the book. I appreciated, as well, the skillful work of Mary Ann Thompson in the final editing. And always, thank you to Grant for ongoing advice and encouragement.

AUTHOR'S NOTES ABOUT THE IRISH WORDS IN THE STORY

Cuchulain (pronounced koo **kull** en) is a great hero in Irish legends. Many stories have been written about his brave deeds. Dogs play an important role in the legend. One of the stories tells how Cuchulain himself came to be known as the 'Hound of Culann'. In this novel, however, the two wolfhounds are newly imagined.

Samhain (pronounced **sau** win) refers to October 31, the end of the harvest season and the beginning of winter.